TROUBLED TIDINGS

A CHRISTMAS NOVELLA

VANISHING RANCH
BOOK 8

CHRISTY BARRITT

CHAPTER
ONE

"EIGHTEEN-YEAR-OLD JACOB CARLSON has been missing for ten days now." A female newscaster's voice floated through the speaker on Dean Burns's phone. "He went for a hike in the Mojave Desert and hasn't been seen since."

Didn't people know they should never hike alone? Dean shook his head as he traveled down the lonely road in his truck. He hoped someone found the missing guy. What a terrible ordeal his family must be going through.

"Also, beware of the Roadside Bandits who have been hitting the area for the past two months," the newscaster continued. "It's been a few days since they were known to be active, which means they're due to strike again. Who would do this at Christmastime, you might be wondering? That's what we'd all like to know also. Anyone with information, please contact . . ."

"How can you even listen to that?" Kota Perez glanced over at him from the passenger seat.

He shrugged. "What can I say? I guess I like to stay informed, Miss Kota."

"How about staying informed about good things instead?"

"That's a great suggestion. I'll take it under consideration."

She raised her eyebrows. "Those people remind me of the bandits in the Wild West that I've always heard about—the ones who robbed stagecoaches."

"That sounds about right."

Dean tapped his screen, and the reporter's voice disappeared.

He'd downloaded the local newscast to listen to on the drive. He could see that was a mistake. Instead, he hit another button and "I'll Be Home for Christmas" filled his red F150 instead.

Much better.

In some ways, this stretch of desert felt like America's final frontier. It was still untamed with its own brand of justice.

Kota shifted beside him, crossing her jean-clad legs as she got comfortable. "I was reading a book the other day about the Old West, and the author talked about how rich people traveling from the East actually *wanted* to get robbed when they came out for a visit. It became somewhat of a rite of passage. They'd even get their pictures taken with the robbers so they could show the photos to their friends at home. Isn't that crazy?"

Dean smiled, enjoying hearing her talk. Their conversations had been pretty generic since they'd met eight months ago. Mostly, they talked about cooking and cleaning—since that's what he and Kota did for a living.

They saw each other almost every day, but so far he only knew a few things about her. She mostly kept to herself.

But he liked getting to know her better. He really liked hearing her talk about something other than work. Maybe she was finally coming out of her shell.

"Yes, the whole situation with the Roadside Bandits is crazy," he finally said. "I try to stay away from trouble. I definitely don't invite it into my life."

"Smart man." Kota rubbed her arms and stared out the window as the sun began to sink lower in the sky. Maybe they'd get a pretty sunset tonight. There was nothing like a desert sunset with its layers of rich colors.

The barren landscape stretched for miles and miles around them. The road ahead of them wound through the land like a piece of Christmas garland that had been abandoned.

The last car they'd passed had been twenty miles back.

This area was truly off grid.

Dean, originally an Alabama boy, loved it here in western Arizona. The landscape was ever changing. Sometimes flat. Sometimes hilly. Sometimes cut with dry canyons. Sometimes there was no foliage, and sometimes the landscape was dotted with sagebrush and agave or Joshua trees.

He often felt as if he'd been transported to another world out here.

Vanishing Ranch, where he worked as chef, was in the middle of nowhere—for good reason. But that meant he had to drive three hours to get to the specialty store to find the ingredients he needed for Christmas dinner. Then they had to drive another three hours on the return trip.

He and Kota still had an hour and a half until they'd be back at the ranch.

Sure, there were closer stores. But to get exactly what he needed, he'd had to go farther.

It was time consuming, but he was glad he had company on this trip.

He glanced at Kota as she studied a picture in her hands.

He grinned when he saw it.

Someone on the sidewalk outside the grocery store had been offering Polaroid photos in front of a cactus decorated with Christmas lights. Dean had insisted the two of them have a picture taken together. He'd made a nice donation to the vagabond who'd been trying to raise some money. He liked to help others whenever he could.

In the photo, Dean stood with one arm around Kota and the other offering a thumbs up while Kota grinned sweetly as she tilted her head at the photographer.

The woman had always reminded him of Salma Hayek with her pleasant features, slim frame, and long, dark hair.

She was beautiful and sweet with a killer smile.

But he could also see the pain behind her eyes, and he knew there was more to her story.

There was more to everyone's story, wasn't there? His included.

"So, are you happy now?" Kota lowered the picture, leaving it on the seat between them. "You have the ingredients for that turkey-fluffin you've been talking up for the past several weeks."

"Turducken," he corrected. "Turkey-duck-chicken."

Yes, he'd been talking it up at the ranch. He loved

discussing food because food bonded people, and eating meals together at a common table helped to build community. He saw his job as a ministry of sorts.

Kota cast a smile his way. "You're really going all out for your Christmas meal. Doesn't it take like five or six hours to prepare the tur-duffin?"

"Turducken." He chuckled. "Yeah, about that long, and another twelve hours to roast it."

"I can't imagine."

"I roast it at a hundred fifty degrees. Comes out juicy and tender. Only the best for the residents at Vanishing Ranch." That's what he always told himself.

The guests there had been through awful experiences, and Dean wanted to do everything he could to ensure they'd enjoy a nice Christmas at their new home away from home. Whatever he could do to help . . .

Christmas was tomorrow. Yes, tomorrow. He'd intended on buying everything he needed earlier in the month. But things had been busy with several new residents joining them—the holidays seemed to bring out the worst in some people—and Dean hadn't had a chance to get away.

He was grateful Kota had blessed him with her company on the trip. Really, she'd come out of convenience. There were a few things she'd wanted to pick up in town also, so she'd caught a ride.

Dean wasn't complaining.

No woman had turned his head—not since his sweet Angelica had died from cancer three years ago. But there was something fascinating about Kota. She never wanted any attention for herself, she never complained, and she always seemed grateful.

His mama used to say that a person couldn't be sad and grateful at the same time. As usual, his mama was right.

Just as they were about to round a bend in the desolate road, a pop sounded.

The next instant, his truck began to bounce.

His steering wheel fought against him, jerking to the side.

His jaw tightened. "You've got to be kidding me . . ."

Kota's eyes widened with alarm as she glanced at him. "What is it?"

He frowned before bringing his truck to a stop and throwing it in Park. "I think I just blew a tire."

"What?" Her voice caught as she looked around at the landscape.

The landscape devoid of civilization.

"Stay here." He opened his door and stepped out.

The fifty-degree late afternoon greeted him. Right

now, it was calm outside, but forecasters were calling for some unseasonable weather later. That was just another reason he wanted to get back to the ranch as soon as possible.

Dean walked toward the back of his truck, shaking his head as he anticipated what he'd find.

Sure enough, his tire was flat as a pancake.

How in the world had that happened? His tires had plenty of tread left on them. He routinely maintained the correct air pressure.

He always took care of his vehicles. Maybe it was his military background. His years of service had turned him from an unmotivated teen into a disciplined soldier. Those traits served him well now.

He shook his head, his hands on his hips as he made his way back to his door. The song on his phone had changed, and now "Rockin' Around the Christmas Tree" drifted out—such a cheery tune for the moment.

He leaned inside toward Kota. "Turns out we do have a slight problem—a flat tire. Thankfully, I have a spare in the back, but it's going to take a few moments to fix it."

She had her phone out and squinted as she stared at it. "Unfortunately, we don't have a signal out here."

Dean wasn't surprised. Many areas in the middle of the desert had no cell phone service.

"We'll be okay," he told her. "Let me just get this tire changed, and we'll be on our way."

He reached into the truck and cut the engine, shoving the keys into his pocket. He wanted to conserve all the gas he could.

But as he started toward the back of the truck, he paused.

In the far distance, he spotted another vehicle heading their way.

Maybe the newscast he'd just been listening to was messing with his mind because Dean wasn't usually one to jump to ominous thoughts.

But when he saw two men hanging out from the truck bed, a bad feeling began brewing in his gut.

He had a feeling these guys wouldn't be stopping to help them.

No, they'd stop to start trouble.

CHAPTER
TWO

KOTA STARED AT HER PHONE, waving it in the air as if the action might magically give her a signal.

She knew it wouldn't.

Something about the desert had always frightened her.

She'd looked it up one time, and there was actually a name for it. Eremophobia. Fear of the desert.

At least, she knew she wasn't the only one who wasn't fond of empty, wide-open spaces.

Even though she'd grown up in Mexico in a climate similar to this, there had been civilization around her back in her hometown. A village filled with family and friends.

At ten, she'd moved to the US. But Mexico still seemed like home.

Ever since she'd come to Vanishing Ranch, she'd avoided these wide-open spaces. She didn't like feeling so exposed. She needed more security, more containment.

She hadn't always been like this. But once, her ex-boyfriend had dropped her in the middle of the desert as punishment and left her there for two days without food or water. Eventually, he'd come back to find her—giving her a grim warning about what would happen next time if she disobeyed him.

When she still couldn't get a signal, a sense of unease filled her.

She knew Chef was entirely capable of changing the tire and getting them home. Even though the man was a cook, he was strong with broad shoulders, a fit build, and impressive muscles.

He wasn't the type of man she'd want to run into in a dark alley. In fact, he had frightened her at first because of his large, intimidating size.

But when Kota had gotten to know him, she'd realized Chef was truly a sweetheart—the kind of person who would give someone the shirt off his back. He had dark skin, a nearly bald head, a bright smile, and an easygoing manner. He could talk to anyone, and he made all the women at the ranch feel like long-lost family.

Other than his cooking skills and friendly

demeanor, Kota didn't know much about him. Once or twice, she'd heard him mention his wife, who was now deceased. *Angelica.*

Chef always said her name with such fondness.

Kota couldn't imagine what that would be like to lose a spouse. She'd been married once until her husband had left her for another woman. But Carlos had never been that affectionate or warm—or even that respectful—so it wasn't exactly a huge loss.

Then she'd fallen into the arms of Freddy Martinez.

She fought a frown at the thought of her ex-boyfriend.

At first, Freddy had been charming and charismatic, and dating him had been exciting. She'd realized too late that there was entirely more to him, however. He had a malicious side that emerged over time.

Kota rubbed her jaw, still remembering what it had felt like the first time he'd punched her. She'd sunk against the wall in disbelief.

Then he'd convinced her it was a one-time instance and wouldn't happen again.

She'd been wrong to believe him.

For two years, he'd manipulated her into staying with him. Made her believe that she was better off with him than without. That each time he hit her it was somehow her fault. That she was lucky he put up with her.

She didn't see a way out.

Until a chance meeting changed everything . . .

Chef—that was what everyone at the ranch called Dean—suddenly opened her door and snapped her from her thoughts.

His concerned expression made her muscles tighten with worry.

"We might have trouble." His voice sounded grim as his gaze locked with hers.

Alarm raced through Kota as his words sank in. "What do you mean?"

He nodded toward a vehicle coming up behind them.

Another vehicle? That was good news . . . right?

Yet she knew it wasn't.

Still, she asked, "They should be able to help, yes?"

What was she missing here? There was clearly more to this story.

Chef grimaced, apprehension in his gaze. "I wish I could say that. But I'm nearly certain that hole didn't appear in my tire by accident. I found some nails on the road about ten yards back. Someone left them there, hoping this would happen."

The blood drained from Kota's face.

She remembered that report about the Roadside Bandits they'd heard on the newscast.

Was that who was coming toward them right now?

Alarm raced through her.

Her gaze locked with Chef's as fear made her quiver. "What are we going to do?"

He glanced behind them again. As Kota followed his gaze, she noted that the truck was less than a half a mile away. They didn't have much time.

"We can't stay here." He rubbed his hardened jaw, his gaze turning all business. "We'll be sitting ducks. Grab your things. We need to move."

"What?" Kota was certain she hadn't heard him correctly.

Was he overreacting? Being paranoid?

The serious expression on his face made it clear he wasn't joking.

"We don't have much time," he repeated. "We need to go."

Quickly, Kota scrambled from the truck. She shoved her phone and wallet into her back pockets. She hadn't brought a purse with her.

Her lungs suddenly felt uncomfortably tight.

"Bring your coat." Chef reached inside then thrust the black jacket into her hands before grabbing his phone. "It's going to get cold."

He thought they'd be out here for a while, didn't he?

Kota didn't like the sound of that.

She slipped on her coat and zipped it.

Then Chef grabbed her hand and tugged her away as the truck sped toward them.

———

Dean tried not to show how alarmed he felt.

But he didn't know how this situation would turn out.

He prayed he was overreacting. He'd take the embarrassment of that any day to the ominous danger that could be racing toward them.

As he quickly tried to formulate a plan, he glanced around.

Out here, there was nowhere to hide from those men. The sagebrush and cacti wouldn't offer much protection.

But they had to try.

They didn't have much choice right now.

Even though the landscape was fairly flat, hills rose in the distance. If he remembered correctly, a dry canyon bed cut through the ground about a half mile from here.

If he and Kota could make it there, maybe they could find shelter until this situation passed.

Hand in hand, they began sprinting across the desert.

The truck was getting closer by the moment.

"Chef . . ." Kota said as they ran.

He barely slowed up as he glanced her way. "Are you okay, Miss Kota?"

She stopped and leaned forward, her palms resting above her knees as she caught her breath. "I'm . . . scared."

He paused as concern pulsed through him. "That's understandable. We just need to keep moving right now. Okay?"

As he glanced back at the approaching truck, he saw it had veered off the road. It was now headed straight for them, picking up speed with every tire rotation.

Dust billowed behind the truck in thick clouds as it bounced over the desert.

The guys in the back hollered, clearly wanting to let Dean and Kota know trouble was headed their way.

Dean glanced at the hills in the distance, wondering if they'd make it to the canyon in time. Clearly, the truck wouldn't be able to follow them into the gulch.

Heading there was Dean and Kota's only option right now.

"We've got to go faster. You can do this. Okay?"

She looked up, her gaze haggard, before nodding. "Okay."

He took her hand and began sprinting again.

Kota ran with him. Every once in a while, he heard a grunt or gasp escape.

Dean glanced at the truck one more time.

It was getting close.

Too close.

If they didn't move faster, the vehicle would overtake them.

Just as the thought raced through his head, a shot cut through the air.

A bullet, he realized.

These guys were firing.

The men in the back of the truck let out a victorious roar.

Disgust churned in Dean's stomach.

These guys enjoyed making others feel fear.

That made them even more dangerous.

His muscles went taut.

Dean had to get Kota to safety.

He had to get her there now.

CHAPTER
THREE

KOTA COULDN'T LET Chef know how winded she felt. Nor did she want to express how quickly her heart was beating or how sweaty her palms felt.

No doubt, Chef already knew that last detail since he gripped her clammy hand with his large one.

But she knew if she slowed down, these guys would catch them. That one of their bullets might pierce her skin. Chef's skin.

Out here, there was no one to help them.

Without a cell phone signal, they had only themselves to depend on.

She heard the truck behind them. Heard it getting closer. Heard the guys inside hooting and hollering.

Those men were enjoying taunting them.

Their heartlessness terrified her.

What would those guys do if they caught up with her and Chef?

She didn't want to think about it.

"Not much farther." Chef squeezed her hand harder as he pulled her forward.

But he was being optimistic. Those hills—where she assumed they were heading—still looked incredibly far away.

Especially as her muscles tensed and her chest tightened.

Kota was only in her early forties, but she'd never felt so out of shape.

Somehow, maybe miraculously, she and Chef reached the hills—and the canyon that cut deep into them just beyond the knolls.

Chef paused at the edge, surveying it a moment. "It's probably eighteen feet down. I think we can make it. Let's try."

Her head spun as she glanced down. This seemed like something they would need rappelling gear for.

But she was going to have to trust Chef right now. She had no other choice.

He climbed down a few steps first and then took her hand to help guide her.

Her entire body quaked as she navigated the steep, rocky path.

Halfway down, she heard the vehicle above them

rumble to a stop. Heard doors opening and closing. Heard men talking.

More fear raced through her.

She and Chef weren't at the bottom yet. From here down, the walls jutted out.

If they climbed down any farther, they'd be exposed.

At least, a slight overhang protected them now.

As another shot split the air, Chef's arm darted out in front of her. He pressed her against the rock facing, holding her in place. His trademark gold watch glinted in the fading sunlight.

Kota's heart thrummed in her ears. She waited, unclear how many men were up there or if they'd come into the canyon to grab them.

"You think you can get away?" one of the men called. "That's wishful thinking."

"We're coming for you," another said in a mocking voice. "This is going to be fun . . . well, not for you two."

Her lungs tightened.

Why hadn't those guys simply stolen Chef's truck? Or looked for valuables inside and then left? Wasn't that what robbers did?

It seemed they wanted something directly from Chef and Kota.

The thought of that struck terror in her.

But she couldn't look to see what was happening out there. Not right now.

All she could do was wait.

But the dreams she'd had of a cozy Christmas at Vanishing Ranch seemed to be disappearing faster than Santa and his reindeer flying into the night.

———

Dean continued to press Kota against the wall, his heart racing.

These guys hadn't gone after his vehicle. From what he understood, that's what the Roadside Bandits usually did.

They terrorized those inside before taking any valuables. Of course, most people didn't leave valuables in their vehicles—they carried them with them. Things like jewelry and wallets.

But the fact that these guys were both openly chasing them and shooting sent up major alarms.

Although . . . Dean wasn't sure the men were actually shooting to kill. If they were, they were terrible shots.

Maybe these guys just wanted to scare him and Kota.

He didn't know.

But he didn't like it.

"You going to come out and make this easy for us?" one of them shouted. "Come out, come out, wherever you are."

"This is like a game of hide-and-seek," another said. "It was always my favorite."

Several more blasts split the air, and Kota muffled a scream beside him. Dean felt her heart beating against his arm as he leaned into her.

He wished he could take away her fear.

But he couldn't.

Not right now.

All he could do was protect her.

He frowned.

This was supposed to be a simple outing.

Please, Lord. Don't let it turn any uglier than this. Please—not for my sake but for Kota's.

Suspicious silence stretched through the air, and he waited.

What were those guys doing now? Were they coming down into the canyon to shoot them? Or did they have other more sinister plans?

Dean's heart beat harder at the thought.

He waited, poised to act if necessary.

Several minutes passed, and nothing happened. The men with all their obnoxious comments had gone quiet.

Finally, he turned toward Kota and put a finger

over his lips to indicate she should remain quiet.

He needed to see what was happening.

She nodded, but her wide eyes made it clear she was terrified right now.

Before he could climb the canyon wall, doors slammed above him.

An engine roared.

Tires spun.

Dean held his breath.

Were those guys leaving?

His heart slowed a moment.

Good. Maybe he and Kota were safe now.

Then he could go back to his truck, change the tire, and they could be on their merry way.

Could this situation really be over?

Cautiously, Dean scaled back up the canyon wall, thankful for the small crevices his large feet somehow managed to fit into. As he climbed, he saw a few bullet casings that had tumbled down the rock wall.

Seeing them was a reminder of how ugly the situation could have been. Thankfully, none of those bullets had hit them.

When he reached the top of the cliff, he carefully peered over the edge. He needed to be certain that those guys hadn't left someone here to keep an eye out for him and Kota.

Only the desert stared back at him.

Relief softened his shoulders a moment.

As he glanced in the distance, he spotted those men. They'd gone back to his truck and surrounded it. No doubt they were pillaging it, searching for anything valuable to steal.

They wouldn't find much. But Dean hoped they would get what they wanted and leave. As far as he knew, these guys didn't usually steal the vehicles, only the things inside. He'd even left the door unlocked so they wouldn't smash his windows.

Once they were gone, Dean could change the tire, and he and Kota could head back to Vanishing Ranch.

Dean continued to watch as the guys climbed back into their truck.

But instead of heading back down the road, the truck made a U-turn.

Those guys were coming toward them again.

What?

Dean's spine stiffened with alarm.

Why would these guys come back for them?

Did they think they could get the truck key from him?

He didn't know.

But he didn't like this.

AS CHEF BEGAN to climb back down toward Kota, she saw the unease on his face and knew something was wrong.

He paused on the narrow ledge beside her, and his gaze locked with hers. "They went over to my truck for a few minutes. But now they're coming back this way."

The breath left her lungs.

Certainly she hadn't heard him correctly.

"What?" The word squeaked from her lips.

Chef nodded, his jaw hard. "We need to keep moving. I don't know what these guys are planning, but we have to take every precaution. There's no law and order out here, Miss Kota."

Miss Kota. He always called her that, even though she was only a few years younger than he was. He called all the women at the ranch by "Miss," claiming once that it was a Southern term of endearment.

"Even if the authorities routinely patrolled out here," Chef continued, "by the time help arrived, it would be too late."

Kota nodded. Chef was right. They needed to get to safety. Right now, they had a slight head start. But that advantage wouldn't last long.

Chef instructed her on every step as they climbed farther down the wall into the canyon. Parts were rocky. Other parts jutted out. Her feet nearly slipped several times.

But with Chef guiding her, Kota had remained steady.

Above them, more doors slammed. More footsteps sounded. More crude comments cut through the air.

Finally, she and Chef reached the bottom of the yellowish-brown canyon, and shadows from the deep walls surrounded them.

Kota let out a breath, feeling a small sense of victory.

They'd done it.

They'd made it down here.

Then Kota glanced up.

Her sense of accomplishment vanished.

Her heart quickened.

Four men glared down at them.

She lowered her gaze as if that might help conceal her. Chef moved closer, his frame towering over her.

But none of that happened quickly enough.

"Kota?" one of the men called. "Is that really you?"

Her heart lodged in her throat as panic raced through her.

Was that . . . Langston?

Freddy's best friend?

If these guys were friends with Freddy, then they truly were evil.

Langston let out a long, low chuckle. "I thought that was your picture I saw in the truck. How fortuitous. I was hoping we'd run into you again one day."

———

Every muscle in Dean's body went rigid as he listened to the men and their lewd comments.

How in the world did these guys know Kota's name?

She knew something about these guys, didn't she? Because she'd been pale before, but now she almost looked like a ghost.

There was *clearly* more to this story.

But he didn't have time to figure out those details now. They had to concentrate on survival.

He glanced at Kota as they stood at the base of the narrow canyon. "We've got to keep moving."

Kota's gaze snapped toward him as she seemed to come out of her state of shock. She quickly nodded, even though her eyes still appeared glazed and hollow.

Wasting no more time, the two of them took off in a run again, traveling deeper into the sandstone canyon.

Thankfully, it wasn't rainy season, so flash flooding wasn't much of a threat. However, the weather had been crazy lately.

Forecasters had said something about La Niña or some other weather system that was currently affecting the area. Even though it was in the fifties outside right now, they'd had some seventy-degree days lately as well as other days when the temperature dropped into the thirties.

None of that mattered right now. Only getting to safety did.

Dean heard the men above them. They made no secret about their presence as they kicked rocks, talked, shouted, and occasionally fired their weapons. If he had to guess, those guys had been drinking.

Dean would figure out the rest once he knew these guys were no longer on their tail.

As they continued to weave between the rocky walls, Dean glanced at the sky and realized they probably only had about two more hours of daylight.

As soon as the sun dipped below the horizon, the temperature would also drop.

They'd have even more challenges ahead of them.

For now, they just needed to move.

Dean had never been to this canyon before, but he'd talked about planning a trip out this way. Jesse Marx, one of the operatives at Vanishing Ranch, was going to come with him so they could explore. They'd even looked at some maps together.

If Dean remembered correctly, this canyon ended after about a half mile and spilled out into the desert.

That could be a death wish.

More yells sounded behind him.

Those guys were still coming after them.

They were getting closer.

His spine stiffened at the thought.

Just then, more gunfire rang out. He didn't think they were shooting to kill.

They were shooting to make a statement.

These guys wanted to taunt him and Kota. The men wanted to let him and Kota know that they were in danger. They wanted them to feel fear.

It was working.

As Dean glanced back, he saw how pale Kota's face had gone.

Her fear was real right now.

Did these guys know her? How did that guy know her name?

Had they targeted Kota for some reason?

Were they waiting to ambush his truck in particular?

So many questions raced through his head.

But those details were unimportant right now.

Dean just needed to concentrate on keeping Kota alive and out of these guys' hands.

A few minutes later, he realized his assumption about the canyon was correct.

The gulch ended, and a wide-open stretch of land waited in front of them.

The exposed area meant there was nowhere else to hide without going back into the canyon . . . and right toward the gunmen pursuing them.

As soon as she saw the open expanse before them, Kota froze so quickly she nearly toppled forward.

"How is it possible that this canyon simply

ends?" she muttered. "What are we going to do now?"

Kota glanced up at Chef. He seemed stunned also as he stared at the landscape in front of them.

He said nothing.

She expected him to ask questions about the fact that one of the guys had known her name. But he didn't.

Those would come soon enough. She'd need to share why those men had recognized her.

How they'd known her name.

They were *Freddy's* friends.

They fit the profile.

Freddy had always liked to keep company with people who enjoyed striking terror in others.

But those guys couldn't have been specifically looking for her.

Too much time had passed since she'd left Freddy.

The fact they'd found her was . . . a coincidence. It had to be.

Even though Freddy lived three hours from here, he might consider this stretch of desert his territory. He was a crime lord who had his hands in multiple criminal activities. He'd always been trying to expand his enterprises.

No doubt, nothing had changed in the two years since Kota had last seen him.

Unless things had gotten even worse.

The more territory Freddy gained, the more powerful and evil he grew.

In fact, she tried not to come out this way often simply because coming this way meant coming closer to where Freddy was headquartered.

When she'd heard about the Roadside Bandits on the ride back to the ranch earlier, she'd never imagined she might know them. But they could definitely be Freddy's guys.

Why hadn't she considered the possibility earlier?

Probably because she tried to forget about that part of her life. She hadn't been able to forgive herself for what had happened during that time. Seeing Freddy's guys only reminded her of that.

Chef shifted and drew in a deep breath as if he'd made up his mind.

"Come on." Chef pulled her from the canyon. "This way."

They did a U-turn and began travelling back in the same direction they'd come from—but on top of the canyon this time.

"Is this safe?" Her voice trembled as she asked the question.

"It's the best option we've got right now."

Kota swallowed hard and nodded.

At least, it wasn't totally flat up here. A few rocky formations dotted the area. Maybe those would protect them when the other guys emerged.

A touch of hope stirred inside her.

Kota wished she and Chef could somehow circle back to his truck and take off. But she knew it wasn't a possibility. Even if they were able to get back, they still had a flat tire to contend with.

As they ran, the lyrics to "God Rest Ye Merry Gentlemen" suddenly began playing in her mind.

Remember Christ our Savior was born on Christmas Day. To save us all from Satan's power when we were gone astray. Oh, tidings of comfort and joy . . .

Comfort and joy? Those two concepts nearly felt foreign to her at times. Because she'd definitely gone astray in the past.

Kota often struggled with forgiving herself. She'd known about some of the criminal activities Freddy was involved with. Maybe she should have tried harder to stop him.

She could have done *something*.

Then again, Freddy probably would have killed her if she had.

Needless to say, for most of her adult life—but especially since she'd left Freddy—Kota hadn't felt any kind of comfort or joy.

But the meaning of the song had always been beautiful to her and had drawn her into a place of contentment.

"Hey!" A shout pulled her from her thoughts.

A shout followed by another gunshot.

"Stop right there or I'll shoot!"

Without turning, Kota knew one of the men had emerged from the canyon and spotted them.

CHAPTER
FIVE

DEAN PAUSED, turned, and stepped in front of Kota as the gunman came into view and faced them.

Adrenaline, along with a surge of protectiveness, filled him.

"Thought you'd outsmart us, did you? We figured you'd try something like this, and I climbed up a little early. Good thing I did." The man smirked. "My friends will be coming along in just a few minutes."

Dean stared at him. The guy had dirty, unkempt blond hair, an unshaven face, and he wore dusty jeans with a smudged white T-shirt.

But mostly, Dean noticed the look in his eyes.

This guy was enjoying this.

The good news was that it sounded like the man in front of them now was the only one up here. The rest of the gang must still be searching the canyon. But this guy had said they'd be coming along soon.

That could work in their favor.

But this guy had a gun, and Dean didn't. Sometimes he would conceal carry, but he knew that Kota didn't like guns. She'd made a comment about it once as she'd helped him fix breakfast when he wasn't feeling well. Because of that, Dean hadn't brought one with him on this trip.

That could turn out to be a fatal mistake.

"So . . . you're Freddy's girl, huh?" The man's eyes twinkled.

Dean squinted.

Freddy? Who was Freddy?

"He still has your picture on his desk. Do you know what Freddy's gonna say when we tell him we found you, Kota? He'll be ecstatic. Especially when we bring you back with us."

Dean bristled at the man's words.

That would only happen over his dead body.

He glanced around again, looking for anything he could use to help them right now. He could hear the other men in the canyon. They'd be here soon.

Dear Lord, help us . . . please.

That's when he saw his answer to prayer.

He slowly backed up.

This guy probably thought Dean was trying to retreat out of fear.

But there was so much more to it than that.

"I don't want anything to do with Freddy anymore." Kota's voice trembled as she said the words.

There was *clearly* more to this story.

Dean would worry about those details later.

He didn't like where this confrontation was going.

"Oh, but he wants something to do with you." The man said the words in a singsong voice. "You should already know that no one walks away from Freddy, especially not his girlfriend."

His girlfriend? There was a lot about Kota Dean didn't know.

More questions pummeled him.

"I'm not his girlfriend. I'm my own person." Kota raised her chin. "I choose what I do."

Dean took another step back, tugging Kota with him as his boots scraped the dry ground.

The sun was sinking lower and lower. Maybe they could use that to their advantage.

"He's dated other women since you, of course." The man's singsong tone turned malicious. "But for some reason you're still the one he wants. He talks about you all the time."

"I'll never be with Freddy again. Never." Something deep and strong hardened Kota's voice.

Still, the man smirked.

As he did, Chef took the final step back.

He leaned toward Kota and muttered, "Trust me."

Then he tackled her onto the ground.

"What do you think you're doing?" the man growled.

As the man dove toward them, he brushed the tree-like cactus next to them. It stood at probably eight feet high with drooping branches and prickly but beautiful light green stems.

It wasn't just any cactus.

It was a jumping cholla.

The spines from the plant easily detached from the body of the cactus and tenaciously hooked themselves to the man's face and arms.

He howled in pain.

Just as Dean had planned.

Wasting no time, Dean grabbed Kota's hand, and they began to run.

———

"How did you know that was going to happen?" Kota asked Chef as she gasped in a breath.

Her muscles strained as they darted across the desert.

Behind them, she heard the man struggling and yelling with pain.

He'd have a hard time pulling the barbs from his skin.

At least, she and Chef had bought themselves some time.

"Anyone who's been around here long enough knows to stay away from a jumping cactus," Chef said over his shoulder. "They can tear you up."

A rush of admiration filled Kota. She would have never thought of doing that.

"Smart thinking," she murmured.

"I try." Chef kept pulling her forward.

Kota knew they still weren't safe. They'd lost time during their confrontation with that guy. His three comrades would be here soon.

Then what would she and Chef do?

As Kota gulped in more deep breaths, her steps slowed.

Chef paused and glanced at her. "Are you okay?"

"I am." But her voice sounded raspy, even to her own ears. "It's just . . . this is a lot."

That seemed like the understatement of the year.

She was out of breath. Her legs ached.

Her bones even complained.

She also wished she had some water, but she didn't mention how thirsty she was.

She would simply conserve her energy—what was left of it anyway.

Chef pulled out his phone and held it in the air.

"Still no signal." He frowned.

Kota shouldn't be surprised. But she was disappointed.

As Chef glanced in the distance, his shoulders tensed. "You've got to be kidding me . . ."

Kota followed his gaze and saw what appeared to be a cloud rising on the horizon. A tidal wave of dust.

She froze. "Is that . . . ?"

Chef's expression tightened. "I've never actually seen one myself since I've been in Arizona."

"A haboob." Grimness lined her tone.

That was what locals called the dust storms that sometimes swept through the area, destroying everything in its path. They usually happen during monsoon season in the summer months.

But that didn't mean it couldn't happen in December.

As they were witnessing right now.

Kota's gaze locked with his. "Chef . . . if we're out here when that dust storm hits . . . we won't survive.

We can't breathe that air. The dust and sand will fill our lungs, and . . ."

His jaw hardened. "We need to get to safety."

Just as the words left his lips, the other three men emerged from the top of the canyon probably forty feet away.

As the saying went, their guns were blazing.

Chef took Kota's hand, and they took off in a run . . . again.

CHAPTER
SIX

CHEF WANTED to ask if things could get any worse, but he knew better.

First, a flat tire. Then the Bandits came along. Then the men had just happened to recognize Kota because Kota knew their leader, Freddy.

And now a haboob?

Dean glanced back and saw the storm was getting closer. The winds would be on them in no time.

If these guys didn't kill them, the dust storm could.

The good news was these guys seemed clueless about the danger soon to be upon them. They hadn't even turned to look.

Dean glanced around, looking for anything that might help them. Sure, he and Kota could use their shirts to cover their faces, and that would help some.

But not enough.

"Stop!" One of the men sprinted toward them, his gun haphazardly waving in the air.

Dean pulled Kota faster.

He knew she was tired, and he felt bad to push her so hard.

But her life was on the line right now. Her muscles could recover later.

As a burst of wind swept over them, he realized the storm was at their heels. Really close.

"Come on!" He pulled Kota back toward the canyon, and they climbed down the rocky wall.

The move was risky. Usually, people went to higher ground during these storms.

But Dean thought he'd seen a cave earlier. If he and Kota could somehow slip inside maybe they'd be safe.

"Where do you think you're going?" one of the men yelled from above them.

Dean glanced up.

The guy was close. Too close.

Dean had no choice right now but to keep climbing down into the gulch to find this cave.

He only prayed this risk paid off.

———

Kota's heart raced so fast that she could hardly breathe or think.

She had to fully trust Chef as he pulled her back down into the canyon. She wasn't sure what coming down here would solve.

This place would become a wind tunnel.

In fact, their deaths might be faster down here than up above.

But her energy—both physically and mentally—felt zapped. She couldn't even find the strength to argue. Besides, she had no better ideas.

Her legs trembled as she navigated the treacherous path.

She could hear Freddy's guys scrambling behind them.

She could feel the wind sweeping over them, already bringing bits of dust.

Instinctively, she pulled her shirt above her mouth and nose. She squinted as gritty pieces of sand threatened to block her vision.

Another stronger gust of wind filled the air with more sand.

They had mere seconds before this dust storm completely consumed them.

Dear Lord, I never thought my life would end this way. Thank You for all the good things You've done for me. Thank You for this Christmas season. For sending Your

Son as a baby to earth. Thank You for the help You've already given me.

Most of all, please forgive me for the times I've failed You. For the times I've failed others.

She whispered, "Amen."

Tidings of comfort and joy.

The lyrics and melody filled her mind again.

Could Kota ever forgive herself enough to find the comfort and joy mentioned in the Bible?

She wasn't sure.

As the question lingered in her mind, she heard a yell followed by a thump.

She gasped.

The next instant, one of the men fell from above and landed in the canyon below.

Her heart pounded harder.

As she stared at his lifeless body, dust consumed them until she could see nothing at all.

CHAPTER
SEVEN

DEAN COULD HARDLY SEE. He thought he'd spotted that cave right before the dust consumed the air around them.

But now, everything was a brown, gritty blur.

With his T-shirt pulled over his nose and mouth, he blindly crept forward.

Every step along this ledge was treacherous when he couldn't see anything. One wrong move and . . .

He swallowed hard.

He didn't want to think about that.

As he ran his hand along the canyon wall, he finally felt a dip.

His breath caught.

This was it.

The cave.

He'd found it!

He gripped Kota's hand and led her inside. Wasting no time, he pulled her back into the hollow as far as they could go.

He remained in place, sheltering her for several minutes as he gathered his bearings.

Finally, he felt it was safe to open his eyes.

He released a breath. The dust storm hadn't reached them back in their hiding spot. It swept past the opening instead.

They were okay.

For now, at least.

Kota coughed but otherwise seemed okay.

He stepped closer, still determined to block her from any bursts of wind that might reach them. "It's okay. We're okay."

Her stiff body relaxed—but only slightly. "Really?"

She opened her eyes and blinked several times as if surprised. Then she wiped her fingers beneath her eyelashes as if trying to get the dust out. A fine layer of dirt covered them both—but their filth was the least of their concerns right now.

"You're brilliant," she murmured.

When she lifted her gaze toward him, Dean saw the admiration in her eyes.

He shrugged. "I don't know if I'd say that. I'm just glad we found this when we did."

"It's a God thing."

He grinned. "I like that. Yes, this was a God thing."

The pensive expression returned to her face. "Do you think that guy who fell is dead?"

"It's hard to say. Either way, it's not looking good for any of them who are out here in this."

"No, it's not."

Dean pictured what they might be going through out there. "I can't imagine that they're faring very well."

The sound of the wind—which could get up to seventy miles an hour—howled beside them.

They listened a moment without speaking.

Finally, Kota asked, "How long do you think the storm will last?"

"I can't be sure. Maybe ten minutes. Could be an hour."

Her eyes widened. "An hour? What do we do in the meantime?"

Dean's jaw tightened. "We stay here and wait. That's all we can do."

———

Kota couldn't find words to express her gratitude toward Chef.

Really, the man was brilliant. She meant the words.

If he hadn't found this cave, they wouldn't have survived this ordeal. She felt sure of it.

Now, they just had to pass some time until the dust storm swept by and they could get back to his pickup.

"Tell me something about yourself, Miss Kota." Chef stepped back—as much as he could in such a small space—and leaned against the wall. He stood in a way that blocked her—probably in case Freddy's men showed up.

And she knew what he was doing. He was using this conversation to try to distract her.

She appreciated the gesture. Winning the mental game was half the battle. That's what Charlie Soldier always told her.

Charlie ran Vanishing Ranch, and the woman was a force to be reckoned with. She'd helped so many women and men, yet she never wanted any recognition for it.

"First of all, call me Kota." She pushed a dusty lock of hair out of her eyes, not wanting to imagine what her face looked like. "Please."

He crossed his arms, revealing his gold watch. She was curious about the story behind it, but she hadn't asked. She didn't feel as if she knew Chef well enough to do so.

"And you can call me Dean." His eyes twinkled.

"It's a deal." Kota let out a breath as she thought about his question. *Tell me something about yourself.* "Something about me? Let's see . . . my family and I came to America when I was ten. My parents worked jobs in the service industry—for a hotel down in San Antonio actually."

"Brothers and sisters?"

"None. It was just me and my parents."

Dean paused and studied her face a moment. Questions brewed in his gaze.

She braced herself.

"Do you mind if I ask who Freddy is?" he finally asked.

Instantly, heaviness pressed on her. But after all they'd been through, Dean deserved to know the truth.

The only other person who knew about her past was Charlie.

"He's a guy I dated after my husband left me." Kota frowned and scrubbed a hand over her face. "I was married for twenty years. It wasn't exactly a happy marriage, but it wasn't terrible. Four years after we were married, I had a late-term miscarriage, and the doctor said I wouldn't be able to have kids."

"I'm sorry."

"Everything changed after that. Carlos lost interest in me." She knew if she stopped to think about it too long that she wouldn't be able to finish. "One day, Carlos never came home. It turned out, he was cheating on me with a woman from work. He left me and never looked back."

"Ouch."

A burst of wind reached them, and she squinted. "Yes, ouch. Thankfully, I had only myself to support. But it was a real struggle to make ends meet on just my paycheck. I tried having roommates, working two jobs, only eating ramen noodles—whatever I could."

"Ramen? I don't have to tell you about the nutrition value of that, do I?"

That got a faint smile out of her. "No, you don't."

His expression turned serious. "And then?"

"Then I met Freddy at the hotel where I was working. He was so charming and handsome that I thought I'd hit the jackpot. What I didn't know was that Freddy wasn't a jackpot, but he was the opposite. He basically bankrupted my life—not financially, because I didn't have money. But emotionally and mentally. My self-worth . . . it was destroyed."

Dean's eyes narrowed upon hearing Freddy's name. "Tell me more about this Freddy guy."

Her frown deepened. "He told me he owned his own real estate business. I believed him. I mean, he seemed to have money and influence. He convinced me to quit my job to work for him as his secretary." She paused, an invisible weight pressing on her. "That's when I realized he didn't own a real estate business at all."

"What was it?" Another burst of wind swirled around them at his question.

"He was involved in all these backroom deals. Drugs. Guns. Gambling. Probably some human trafficking. Whatever would make him money." Kota's throat tightened at the memories.

"Sounds like a rough guy. But I'm surprised someone like that would be targeting people on the road. Sounds like he has his hands in enough other things."

"You'd think, right? The thing with Freddy is that he gets bored. He's always looking for the next big thing. The next level of excitement. And his guys . . . they're all morons with no moral compass."

A glimmer of amusement flickered in his eyes before quickly disappearing. "You recognize any of those men?"

"Yes. One of them is Langston, Freddy's best friend. He's not as powerful as Freddy, and he doesn't call the shots. But, if it's possible, he's even more messed up."

"What do you mean?" Dean raised his voice to be heard above the howling wind around them.

Kota blew out a long breath. "I never liked being left alone with that guy. There was just something about the way he looked at me . . ." She shuddered. "But I knew he'd never touch me if I was with Freddy. It would have been a death wish for him."

Dean continued to listen, a touch of anger simmering in his gaze. "How long did you and this Freddy guy date?"

She lowered her gaze, feeling that familiar shame. "Two years. Two long years. Things escalated with him. He was so controlling. But I knew if I left him, I wouldn't have money or a place to live or even any friends. He'd isolated me and made me completely dependent on him."

"What about your family?"

"We were never very close. My father is an alcoholic, so my parents have their own issues."

Dean nodded slowly. "How did you get away from Freddy?"

Her gaze lifted. "Charlie helped me. She gave me a new life. She told me that I could start again somewhere else. Anywhere I wanted. With a new identity.

But I wanted to stay at Vanishing Ranch and help her."

Vanishing Ranch, on the outside, appeared to be a horse rescue. In reality, Charlie and her crew helped people in desperate situations find safety.

Charlie had come into the restaurant where Kota had been eating, had overheard a heated discussion she and Freddy were having in the kitchen, and then pulled Kota aside when she went to the restroom. Charlie had offered to help.

Kota had taken a chance and had gone for it. That decision had changed her life—for the best.

A small grin tugged at Dean's lips. "It sounds like a good fit."

She suddenly felt self-conscious. She never talked about herself this much.

As unease jostled inside her, she realized she needed to change the subject. "Enough about me. How did *you* end up at Vanishing Ranch?"

"Now, that's a long story." A sad smile pressed at his lips. "And I'd love to tell you sometime. I'm not sure I'll have the time right now."

At his words, Kota realized the wind was dying and not nearly as loud now as it had been. This could be their chance to leave.

He nodded toward the opening. "These guys

could still be chasing us. We don't want to waste any time."

Her curiosity grew. More than anything, she wanted to hear more about Dean. She wanted to know how this man had become such a rock.

If the kitchen was the heart of the home, then Dean was the lifeblood of Vanishing Ranch. The place wouldn't be the same without him.

As the wind died, Dean turned toward her. "We can't stay here too long. Just in case Freddy's guys survived, we don't want to wait here for them to find us. There should only be two left—but that's two guys with vengeance and guns."

Apprehension thrummed in her blood. "So what are we going to do? Just keep running and running?"

He rubbed his jaw. "I have another idea. Do you trust me?"

Kota didn't even have to think about her answer. "I do."

"Let's go."

CHAPTER
EIGHT

DEAN HOPED HIS PLAN WORKED. That his memory served him correctly.

He and Jesse had tried to plot out exactly where they might go on their trip.

Somewhere off the beaten path, they'd decided. Somewhere rugged and unexpected.

But they'd never taken that break. There always seemed to be too much to do to waste time having fun. Maybe in the spring, they'd decided.

Or maybe the truth was . . . when Dean took time off, he thought too much about Angelica.

Angelica would have told him not to be so serious. She would have told him he had to loosen up and have some fun sometimes. That life was too short.

Yes, it definitely was too short.

Oh, how he missed her. Angelica had represented all the best parts of him, and she'd given him two wonderful sons. His boys were now married with kids of their own.

Sometimes that part of his life as a family man seemed like yesterday.

Yet other times that part of Dean's life seemed like a distant memory. Like remembering a story told about someone else long ago.

But his story wasn't over yet.

God still had plans for him.

And part of that plan was getting himself and Kota to safety.

Slowly, he crept from the cave and glanced around.

A fresh coat of dust and sand covered the rocks and ground.

As he glanced down, he saw the man that had fallen into the canyon.

He lay there unmoving.

Dean could see from the angle the man had landed that he hadn't survived.

Not that Dean wanted to wish harm on anyone, but he hoped the storm had incapacitated the other two guys—at least temporarily.

He led Kota from the cave, instructing her not to

look below. He didn't think she could handle seeing the dead man there.

When they reached the bottom, they'd head in the opposite direction from last time.

If they could travel along the base of the canyon, maybe they could reach somewhere with cell phone service.

But if they lost time, then they lost daylight. That was something they couldn't risk.

Dean knew the dangers of being out here in the desert at night. They weren't ones that he wanted to face. Temperatures would plummet. Wildlife could be harder to spot. Getting lost was more of a risk.

But they didn't have much choice right now either.

When they climbed to the dried riverbed, Dean's gaze went to the ground.

He wished he was seeing things.

But he knew he wasn't.

There, in the freshly laid dust, was a single set of footprints.

A set of footprints that moved in the same direction he and Kota headed now.

Right then, Dean knew he had a decision to make.

Should he continue forward with his original plan?

Or should he loop back in the opposite direction

where there were miles and miles of nothing as far as the eye could see?

———

Kota saw the wariness on Dean's face.

She followed his gaze and saw the footprints.

Her breath caught.

Those had been left recently. Since the storm had blown through.

A flash of fear traveled down her spine.

At least one of the guys chasing them had survived. Maybe he'd come down here after them and had hidden behind a crevice. Maybe that had provided him with enough protection from the sandstorm that he'd survived.

Now, he was clearly looking for them.

As Dean began walking in the same direction as the footprints, fear pulsed through Kota.

She froze and tugged him back.

They were going to walk right into this guy's hands!

"What are you doing?" Her voice came out slightly breathless.

He turned toward her, the gray sky above them turning darker by the moment. "If we head back toward where the canyon ended, we'll be sitting ducks. Once we're out of the protection of the canyon, there's nothing out there for miles. We have no water. No food. No shelter. And no cell phone service. We can't chance that."

"But if we go back toward where we originally entered the canyon, then we're going in the same direction as this guy. He's just going to kill you. Then he'll take me to Freddy." Her voice quivered with fear.

Dean stepped closer and pushed a lock of hair behind her ear. "I'm not going to let that happen."

A shiver ran down her spine at his touch.

Kota had always been attracted to Dean. Something about him was just so lovable once you got past his intimidating build. But she liked his strength. Liked how safe he made her feel.

Even at the ranch he'd made her feel protected. He made it a point to walk her to her cabana when it was dark outside. He caught a box of cleaning supplies from a high shelf before it toppled down on her. He always made sure she remembered to eat.

But she'd known they didn't have a chance together. Kota was too broken. She'd messed up too much.

However, she loved how tender Dean's eyes looked right now.

"I'm not going to let them get you." He squeezed

her arm again, his touch bringing her comfort instead of fear.

He said the words with such assurance that Kota believed him.

After a moment of hesitation, she nodded. "Okay."

Then they began walking through the canyon again. The walls made her feel both protected and like they were closing in on her at the same time.

She wanted to talk. Wanted to ask more questions.

But she didn't dare.

She needed to save her energy and be on alert right now.

As they walked, she glanced above her at the darkening sky. Daylight was quickly disappearing.

The thought caused a shiver to race through her.

Freddy's two remaining henchmen could be anywhere. Hiding on the ledge above them or behind a rock ahead. The darkness would conceal them.

The darkness could conceal many things, however.

Including Dean and Kota.

Maybe they could slip past anyone who might still be looking for them.

That thought temporarily made her feel better.

But after she and Dean walked about twenty minutes, prickles danced up her spine.

She felt unseen eyes watching her.

Dean must have felt something also because he paused and seemed to brace himself.

A small rock from above tumbled down.

No doubt pushed by an unseen force above.

DEAN DIDN'T KNOW what they were about to encounter.

He had to assume one of Freddy's guys was up there.

Waiting above them with gun drawn and ready to act.

His heart thrummed harder.

He'd known this could be a possibility.

But he'd hoped the chance wouldn't come to fruition.

As he lifted his gaze toward the cliff, he sucked in a breath.

It wasn't one of Freddy's guys standing there.

Instead, a mountain lion stared down on them.

"Dean . . ." Kota followed his gaze before clutching his arm.

"Just stay still." He barely moved his lips as he stared at the creature.

The oversized cat sat as still as a statue as it watched them, practically blending in with the rocks.

Dean knew what the creature was doing.

This was how the cat hunted its prey.

Since they'd been experiencing a drought here in the desert, that meant food was scarce.

Dean and Kota might look like a decent-sized meal to this hungry animal.

He sensed Kota trembling beside him.

There was nothing he could say to reassure her.

Right now, he simply had to wait to see what this mountain lion might do.

"It's like you guys are just standing there waiting for me," a mocking voice called from overhead.

Dean's breath caught.

Moving only his eyes, he looked over and saw one of Freddy's guys standing above them, only six feet from the mountain lion, with a smirk on his face and a gun in his hands.

The man was clueless that a mountain lion was perched above them.

"We all know how this is going to end. Why don't you just hand her over, big guy? You can walk away. We just want the girl."

The big cat swung his head toward the man's voice. Lifted his chin and sniffed the air.

Dean didn't say anything. He remained frozen.

"What's wrong?" the man taunted. "Cat got your tongue?"

Dean raised his eyebrows. Had that guy really just said that?

The man took a step closer, remaining oblivious to the danger he was in.

Just then, the mountain lion sprang to life with a deep, predatorial growl.

———

The scream caught in Kota's throat.

She crouched, her arms flying over her head in an effort to protect herself.

She waited to feel the animal's claws dig into her. To feel his teeth tear her flesh.

But she didn't.

Instead, she heard commotion.

More rocks tumbled from above. Then an untamed snarl sounded.

Followed by a human scream.

Dean? Was Dean okay? Had the mountain lion gotten him?

She pulled her eyes open and saw the cat attacking Freddy's guy instead.

Dean took her hand. "There's nothing we can do for him. We've got to go. Now."

She could hardly breathe as they skirted past the cat. As she heard the howls coming from Freddy's guy.

She'd never forget the agony within the desperate sounds.

But this was their opportunity to get out of here, and the two of them couldn't waste it.

They ran for their lives and didn't look back.

CHAPTER
TEN

DEAN DIDN'T STOP RUNNING until the sound of the mountain lion could no longer be heard.

He didn't want to think about what happened to that man.

He'd had it coming.

But still, Dean didn't like to think of anyone suffering like that.

Maybe this was God's way of watching out for them.

He slowed down and drew in some deep breaths.

There was still one guy out there, but he and Kota needed to pace themselves.

Around them, night had fallen and the cold had deepened.

Dean only hoped that his memory was as good as

he thought it was. He might be nearly fifty, but he was still sharp.

If he was right, in another hour, they'd find somewhere to take shelter.

They just needed to stay safe until they were found.

By now, the crew at Vanishing Ranch should have realized the two of them weren't back yet. They had probably sent out a search party.

Once they found his truck, it would be a matter of trying to figure out which direction he and Kota had gone.

Not long ago during another search operation, the Vanishing Ranch team had gone as far as to use their helicopter to shine a spotlight in the area in order to find someone missing in a similar situation.

Dean knew that Charlie and her gang would do whatever it took to find them also.

But how would the team ever locate them out here?

The closer they got to the truck, the more easily Kota and Dean would be found.

Kota stole a glance at him as they walked through the darkness. "How are you so good at this? I thought you were just a chef?"

He fought a grin.

However, he didn't let down his guard. He

continued to watch everything around them. There could still be more mountain lions.

Anything was a possibility right now.

"Before I became a chef, I worked special operations for the Navy."

Her eyebrows shot up. "You were a SEAL? Like Hudson?"

He chuckled and shook his head. "No, not a SEAL. But I worked alongside the SEALS as a diver."

"So, you were *unofficially* a SEAL?"

His grin widened. "I don't know if I'd say that. But it's a nice sentiment. I was close with them. Those were some great days. Until one of the boats I was on during a mission got bombed."

Her gaze filled with alarm. "What?"

He nodded, instantly sobering. "It was ugly. We all survived. But we didn't come out unscathed." He rubbed his knee.

"You were hurt?"

He shrugged as if it weren't a big deal. "Nearly took out my kneecap. I had to have surgery. I could have gotten out of the military then, but I didn't. I became a chef on an aircraft carrier instead."

Kota cast him another warm glance. "It sounds like you really loved your career."

"I did. The military helped turn my life around—the military and Angelica."

They continued trekking through the dark wilderness.

"Were you married during that time?" Kota asked.

Memories filled him. "Angelica and I were married when I was nineteen. I was a week away from deploying when I met her. It was love at first sight. We saw each other every night that week, and then I left for six months. I knew she didn't know me well enough to wait for me. But she did wait. Two weeks after returning home, I proposed."

Kota blinked. "Wow. That is fast."

Dean nodded. "When you know, you know."

"She must have been a wonderful person."

"The best." His voice trailed with wistfulness. "When I lost her to cancer three years ago, I thought my life was over. Then I realized that wasn't what Angelica would want. I struggled to find a way to reset my life for the first couple of years. Tried to work in a restaurant and then a homeless shelter. Those things were great in their own ways. But when I met Charlie, that's when I knew I'd found my purpose again."

"How did you and Charlie meet?"

They continued walking.

"She was helping someone at the homeless shelter where I was working," Dean said. "I was singing behind the counter as I served food, trying to bring some joy to people, you know? Everyone needs some joy in their lives. Charlie noticed that I knew most of our guests by name, and that they knew me. I guess she saw something in me."

"Who wouldn't?"

He chuckled. "I appreciate that. She left me her card and asked me to call her. Said she wanted to talk about an opportunity."

"You weren't cautious about that?"

"Oh, I was. But I knew who she was. I knew her father was Benjamin Soldier, the football star turned American hero. I was intrigued."

"I can imagine." Kota smiled. "Although, I have to admit, I don't watch football, and I was clueless about who Charlie was when we met."

"That's okay . . . different strokes for different folks, right? Anyway, as they say, the rest is history. I knew as soon as I set foot inside Vanishing Ranch that it was where I was supposed to be."

"That's a beautiful story. We're all blessed to have you there."

Now that the dust storm had passed, the moon moved in and out of the clouds above them. At this moment, the darkness felt astounding—far deeper than anything Dean had experienced down in Alabama.

They reached a part of the canyon that grew narrow and rocky. Navigating it from down here would be tricky—and treacherous.

Dean glanced at the ridge above them. "We should be able to climb out of this, and I'm hoping we'll be able to find help from here."

Kota didn't ask any questions. Dean wasted no time scaling the wall.

But when they reached the top, all he saw was desert.

Despair bit deep inside him.

"I don't see anything. Do you?"

"No. Nothing."

How could he have been so wrong?

———

Kota sensed Dean's disappointment. "Dean?"

He shook his head as he ran a hand over his face. "It's not here."

"What's not here?" She glanced at the vast emptiness around her.

What exactly had Dean been expecting?

He let out a burdened sigh. "I planned a trip out here once, and I remembered seeing the canyon on the map. There was an old, abandoned gold mining town not far from it—probably a mile. It's so far off the beaten path that most people don't even know it's there. It would've given us some shelter and a place to stay until the guys from Vanishing Ranch could find us."

For a moment, Kota forgot her own terror and squeezed his arm. His very muscular arm. "It's okay. We'll figure something else out."

He shook his head, some of the hope disappearing from his gaze. "We can't just keep walking around out here all night. What if those guys come back and find us?"

"It's so dark out here that I doubt that will be the case. If anything, they'll probably pick up their search again in the morning. By then, hopefully, we'll be back at the ranch."

"I was so sure . . ." He ran his hand over his face again.

She squeezed his arm again.

She wanted to do more. To offer an embrace or some other kind of comfort.

But it felt too soon.

Finally, she said, "Let's keep walking. Maybe it's just farther away than you thought."

After a moment of deep contemplation, Dean finally nodded. "Okay."

They began walking side by side.

As the wind swept over them, the cold deepened

and bit into their bones. Kota pulled her coat more tightly around her, thankful Dean had told her to bring her jacket.

But it almost didn't feel warm enough now.

And she was so, so thirsty.

Not that it mattered, but she probably looked like a wreck as well. She had no doubt dust covered her skin and hair. She felt the gritty sand between her teeth.

But they were alive, and she was thankful for that.

"Do you wonder if this is what Mary and Joseph felt like?" Her question rang out into the night.

"What?" Dean glanced at her as if surprised.

"I mean, I like to picture them walking to Bethlehem. I imagine the climate being similar to this. They were probably scared and cold and tired. Who knows? Maybe they even went through a sandstorm."

He let out a little chuckle. "Maybe that detail didn't make it into the Bible story. But I suppose it could have happened."

"And, no, they didn't have gunmen chasing them. But certainly they knew what was at stake. They knew that the task before them would be grueling and heartbreaking."

"But they pushed forward," Dean said.

"That's right. They pushed forward. They believed. They had faith and trusted. That's how I try to live my life as well. I'm not always perfect at it, but I do try."

Dean glanced at her and flashed a soft smile. "I can see that in you, Kota."

"You can?" Surprise rang through her voice.

"I see the way you talk to the ladies at the ranch. I see how much you care for them. How much you put your heart and soul into cleaning up and doing the best that you can with your job. It's admirable."

She shoved a hair behind her ear. "Usually, I don't feel as if anyone sees me."

"Oh, I see you all right." His eyes warmed. "And I know others do too. You just don't seem like the type who wants attention for what you do."

"I don't. I really don't."

"You're doing a good thing at the ranch," Dean said. "Always remember that."

Kota felt herself flush at the sincerity in his voice. "Thank you. So are you."

"I feel blessed to be able to work there."

"Other people are blessed to be around you," she told him.

"I don't know about that."

"I'm serious." She was blessed to be around Dean. He was a bright spot in her day, and Kota found herself making excuses to visit the kitchen so she could see him.

They continued walking for several more moments until finally the clouds drifted and uncovered the moon.

When they did, the light from overhead hit something in the distance.

Something that looked a lot like . . . a ghost town.

DEAN FELT hope flutter in his heart.

This place *was* here. He just hadn't been able to see it.

Kota was right. Sometimes . . . it was just a matter of walking forward in faith. After all, if you could see what you were walking toward then was it really faith that moved you?

He and Kota let out a cry of victory before throwing their arms around each other.

But as Dean held her close, something stirred in his heart.

Something he hadn't felt since Angelica.

Something he wasn't entirely expecting.

He'd been attracted to Kota. She was a beautiful woman.

But he wasn't looking for love or romance. He had been content to be single.

So why did it feel as if something was beginning to change inside him? Was it the circumstances? The danger? The season?

He felt sure it was more than that.

As Kota pulled away from their embrace, she peered up at him. Her eyes were wide, and she appeared breathless, almost as if she felt the same way he did.

Their gazes caught a moment, and something intimate passed between them.

Kota swallowed hard before shoving her hands into her coat pockets. "We found it. I knew we would."

Her words made him smile. "Yes, we did. Now, let's find some shelter. The wind is going to be picking up soon. I can feel it."

"Let's go."

They hurried toward the buildings in the distance.

Dean didn't think that anyone else would be here.

At least, they should be safe for a while.

Still, he prayed the guys at Vanishing Ranch would find them soon.

As they reached the ghost town, Kota stared at it in awe.

It was hard to see much because of the darkness. But as the moon reappeared, it displayed an old town that time had left behind.

For an instant, Kota felt as if she could relate to this place. She felt like the woman who'd been forgotten. Who was aging, whose beauty was fading . . . the one people didn't see anymore.

She shoved aside those thoughts as she studied the town.

There were probably eight different flat-fronted buildings before her. A wooden walkway stretched in front of some of them. Words had been painted atop some of the structures—words Kota couldn't read in the darkness.

They slowly walked down the center of town, a place where Kota imagined disagreements being settled with deadly shootouts. She pictured the gold rush days when people came here seeking fortunes. When fugitives tried to outrun their pasts, and bounty hunters sought their own paydays.

Or maybe she'd just watched too many Westerns in her life. Carlos had loved those shows.

Either way, she was fascinated with this place.

"I've always heard about these old towns." She paused. "Never thought I'd be in one."

"This is pretty fascinating. A real piece of Old West history." Dean nodded slowly, a sense of awe in his gaze.

"I can only imagine what it must have been like for the pioneers to come out here looking for gold. Especially those from the East Coast, where everything is green all the time and the air is humid."

"It must have been surreal, almost like one of us visiting the moon today."

"That's what I always think when I come out in the desert." Kota released a nervous laugh. "I'd rather be here than out in the desert, however."

They paused in the middle of the dirt road, surrounded by rundown buildings.

Kota glanced around. "So which building should we stay in? The jailhouse? Or maybe the old mercantile? Oh, I know. The saloon."

Dean nodded at a building in the distance. "Considering all the talks we've had on our walk, I think that one is appropriate."

"The stable?"

He shrugged and grinned again. "Why not?"

She liked the way he thought. "Works for me."

But as they took a step that way, a noise came from the building beside them.

They both turned in time to see a figure lunging from the shadows.

DEAN BRACED HIMSELF.

Not trouble. Not again.

Had Langston assumed they'd come here and cut them off at the pass?

But as he stared at the man who'd appeared, the guy seemed to be drunk or high. His eyes were bloodshot, and he staggered, hardly able to stand up.

"I thought I heard somebody," the man said with slurred words. "Got any water?"

Was this guy a desert nomad? Someone who wandered from place to place, surviving on whatever he could?

"I'm sorry," Dean said. "But we don't have anything for you."

"How about food?" The man ambled forward on unsteady feet.

"We don't have anything." Dean stiffened as he rose to full height.

"That's too bad. Because you can't stay here unless you can pay me." The man might have sounded tough if he wasn't so strung out and unstable on his feet.

Dean bristled, hoping this guy didn't cause any trouble. "I'm pretty sure you don't own this town."

"Says who? This here's my claim." The man shoved a finger into his own chest. "Possession is nine-tenths of the law, you know."

Dean narrowed his eyes and shook his head. "It doesn't really work like that."

"You wanna fight me for it?"

Dean lifted his chin. "Look, we don't want any trouble."

"That's too bad." The guy fisted his hands. "Because you found it."

Then the man rushed him.

———

Kota held her breath as she watched everything unfold.

The man swung at Dean, but he ducked.

As the guy circled around and lunged at him

again, Dean crouched and flipped the man over his back.

Her eyebrows flew up.

She didn't want to be impressed, but she was.

Dean could not only cook, but he could also fight.

The nomad staggered back to his feet and wobbled as he pointed a finger at Dean. "This isn't over yet."

Then he dove at Dean again.

This time, Dean stepped aside and caught the man in a headlock.

The guy flailed his arms trying to scratch his way out of the hold, but his uncoordinated moves didn't make Dean budge.

"Take it easy, man," Dean said.

The guy didn't slow down.

Kota froze as she anticipated what would happen next.

"Are you going to calm down for me?" Dean asked.

The man continued to struggle. "Never."

"Then we're going to have to do this the hard way."

"What's that supposed to mean?"

"You're about to find out." Dean squeezed the man's neck harder until he finally crumpled to the ground.

Kota sucked in a breath as alarm swept through her. "Is he dead?"

Dean shook his head as he stared down at the man with a touch of pity in his gaze. "No. He just passed out. He'll wake up soon."

A wave of relief washed over her. "What do we do with him in the meantime?"

"Let's get him to some shelter. Maybe when he wakes up, some of the drugs will have worn off."

Dean easily lifted the man over his shoulder and carried him toward the stable. Once inside, Dean propped him against the wall and patted him down.

"No weapons," he muttered.

He reached into the man's pocket and pulled something out. A moment later, he raised his eyebrows and shook his head. "But he does have some cocaine on him."

"Anything else?"

"A wallet."

"Who is this guy?" Kota asked.

"This is the missing hiker. Jacob Carlson."

"What?" Kota's voice lilted with surprise. "He doesn't seem like someone who's in distress. He seems like he's here because he wants to be."

Dean nodded slowly. "I agree. Maybe when he wakes up, he can explain more."

"Maybe his parents will have a merry Christmas

after all. Maybe when the crew from Vanishing Ranch finds us, we can bring him back with us also."

"Let's hope it works out that way." Dean glanced at his watch. "It's only four hours until Christmas Eve is over, and Christmas day is upon us."

They both sat down and leaned against the wall to wait. The scent of days gone by rose around them —dusty and dry. A few tools had been left here— even though he wasn't sure they were old. The shovel and buckets he saw had probably been left by desert wanderers. People came out here on occasion to search for gold at some of the old mines.

"Do you have any special traditions on Christmas Eve or Christmas Day?" Kota glanced up at him.

"Well, I always make turducken." He cast her a glance. "It was my wife's favorite."

"So that's why you want to make it for the ladies at Vanishing Ranch." She touched his arm as realization rolled over her features. "I think that's beautiful."

"Thank you. I just like to do what I can to honor her memory, you know."

"As you should."

He let out a breath. "The first thing my family always did on Christmas morning was to read the Christmas story from the Bible together. Then we'd open presents. We'd give our two boys one thing they want, one thing they need, one thing to wear, and one thing to read. We tried to keep it simple."

"How did your sons like that?"

He let out a soft chuckle. "At the time, they didn't like it so much. Not when their friends got showered with gifts. But I think they can appreciate it now. It taught them some good life lessons. John, my oldest, is an attorney now. Can you believe that? My boy is an attorney? He lives in New York. And my youngest is an engineer for NASA. That blows my mind."

"I know you must be proud of them."

"I'm so proud. Of course, I'd be proud of them whatever they did. I hope you can meet them one day. I just know you would love them too—and their wives and my grandchildren."

A smile slid across her face. "I would like that."

He turned toward her. "How about you?"

She let out a heavy breath. "My family always worked in the service industry. As you probably know, hotels don't close for the holidays. In fact, they're busier than ever. So, we always worked. Whenever we could find time, we'd get together to exchange gifts. My dad saw it as another excuse to drink, which then led to fights. Anyway . . . Christmas was never really a big deal."

"And when you got married?"

Memories pummeled her. "It was more of the

same, really. Now, with Freddy it was different. He wanted to spoil me. To show me what he had to offer if I'd just pretend that he didn't hurt me. It was always extremes with him, you know?"

"I've met that type."

"So, in truth, I've never really had a memorable Christmas." Kota shrugged. "That's okay. I have a job I love and a roof over my head. Who am I to complain?"

"What would your perfect Christmas look like?" He shifted toward her on the ground.

She let out a long breath. "I don't know. It's hard to say. But I think just being with family and enjoying time with them. Sharing laughter and stories. I don't really care about gifts or all the commercial aspects. If someone is going to give me something special, maybe it would be handmade and crafted from the heart, you know?"

"I like that idea."

She cast him a soft smile.

This was all nice to talk about and hope for.

But would either of them really ever get to enjoy Christmas again?

It seemed doubtful.

CHAPTER
THIRTEEN

IF DEAN HAD HIS WAY, Kota would get everything she wanted for Christmas and more.

But, first, they had to get out of here.

He tried to look relaxed, to not show how distressed he felt. But the situation could still turn ugly.

Langston was out there somewhere. He could have followed them.

Even though Dean had kept his eyes open and had remained alert, it was still possible.

For that reason, he had to remain on guard.

Plus, he didn't tell Kota how nervous he was that the gang from Vanishing Ranch may not be able to find them. Those searches in the desert . . . they were grueling. There was so much land to cover. Even with a drone, it would be challenging.

There were so many unknown variables here. It all made him very uncomfortable.

"Tell me about your watch." Kota nodded at his arm.

He glanced at his wrist. "It was my dad's."

"Was it? I think that's great that you still wear it. Were the two of you close?"

"I wish we could have been closer." Dean felt heaviness press on him as the memories flooded back. "The fact is I gave my dad a hard time. I wasn't easy when I was a teen. Dad was always riding my case, telling me that I could be better and that I couldn't succumb to the pressures around me. We didn't have a lot of money. I was hanging out with the wrong crowd, and he could see it. I couldn't."

"So what happened?"

"He told me I either had to join the military or get out of the house." Dean frowned. "I had nowhere to go. Sure, I could live with my friends. But I guess deep down inside, I knew what that would mean—trouble. So I joined the military. The day I left, he gave me his watch, so I'd always know he was thinking about me."

"That's nice."

Dean's jaw tightened as he tried to hold back his emotions. "While I was away at boot camp, he passed away suddenly. Had a heart attack."

"Oh, Dean . . . I'm so sorry."

"I wish he could have seen that all those prayers he lifted for me weren't in vain . . . I turned out okay."

"You turned out more than okay. I'm sure he was proud of you."

"I hope so. I just wish I could go back and change things."

"I think we all feel that way. I know I sure do."

As the man leaning against the wall began to stir, Dean braced himself.

He hoped Jacob wouldn't cause any more trouble . . . but considering their luck so far today, he couldn't count on that.

———

Kota froze as she waited to see what might happen.

Dean bristled beside her.

Jacob moaned before rubbing his head and blinking several times. Finally, he seemed to spot them.

He tensed and drew back, seeming to instantly sober.

"What happened? Where am I? Who are you?" The questions flew from his lips.

Dean raised his hand to slow the man's thoughts. "You attacked us, remember?"

Jacob let out another moan and closed his eyes. "No, I don't actually remember much. I haven't had any water in at least two days. I ran out."

"You're the missing hiker," Dean said. "Your family is worried about you."

"No, they're not." A shadow crossed Jacob's eyes.

"Yes, they are," Dean continued. "They've been all over the news talking about you. Asking for information on your whereabouts. Begging the public for help."

"I find that hard to believe." He lowered his gaze as shame filled it. "Especially after what I've done."

Kota frowned at the defeat in the young man's words. "Whatever you've done, I'm sure they'll forgive you."

"No, they won't. I stole money from them for drugs." He shook his head before letting it drop against the wall behind him. "I couldn't seem to stop myself. I knew they needed that money. It's not like we're loaded. My dad was so angry when he found out."

"What happened?" Kota's heart pounded into her chest as she waited to hear more of his story.

He shrugged, but pain marred his words. "I said some hurtful things. Said I never wanted to see them again. I left and started walking. I eventually ended up here. By the time I realized I was lost, I knew it was too late. I was out here in the middle of nowhere, and no one was going to find me."

"We found you," Kota reminded him.

"No offense, but I'm not sure you are going to be much help. It looks like you two have seen as much trouble as I have." He gave them a pointed look before his eyelids drooped. His burst of energy and coherency seemed to vanish as quickly as it had appeared.

As Jacob's words hung in the air—undisputed—a shadow appeared in the doorway.

Kota gasped.

It was Langston.

He'd found them.

And he had a gun.

CHAPTER
FOURTEEN

DEAN FELT himself bristle as he rose to his feet. "Stay here. I'll handle him."

"I wouldn't be so sure about that," Langston muttered. "I've come too far to lose Kota now."

"How did you even find us here?" Dean stepped closer, his gaze on the man's gun.

He smirked. "I'm good at being sneaky."

"Sneaky like a snake . . ." Kota muttered behind him.

Dean quickly glanced at Jacob. The teen had passed out again and lay unconscious against the wall.

Dehydration must have gotten to him—dehydration and the drugs.

He could see Jacob was still breathing, but Dean

didn't know how much longer that would be the case. He needed help.

"We can make this easy or hard," Langston muttered, twirling the gun on his finger as if it were a toy. "I can shoot you and take Kota, or you can just let me have her and I'll be on my way. I can just leave you here to die."

"You're not touching her." Adrenaline thrummed through Dean's blood.

"Okay, have it your way then." Langston stopped twirling his gun and tried to grip it.

Before he could, Dean lunged at him.

The gun fired.

Kota screamed.

Everything happened in a blur around him.

She'd better not have been hit.

He grabbed Langston's arm and twisted it.

He needed to get that gun from him.

But Langston gripped the Glock more tightly than Dean had assumed he would.

Still struggling, the two of them tumbled out onto the dusty street.

Dean had to subdue this guy before he reached Kota.

That was his only goal.

He'd do whatever it took to make it happen.

———

Kota could hardly breathe as she watched the fight.

The two men had tumbled outside, and she could no longer see them.

She wanted to step closer. Wanted to see what was happening.

But she knew Dean would want her to stay inside the stable.

Dear Lord . . . please. Help him!

She stood and pressed herself into the rough wooden wall behind her. As she glanced beside her, she spotted an old shovel. Maybe if she could grab that . . .

Fear tried to freeze her, but she forced herself to move.

She'd only taken one step toward the shovel when she heard something behind her.

She turned and saw a man step from the shadows of the stable.

Freddy.

Kota's throat tightened so quickly she could hardly breathe.

He wore a smirk on his handsome face as he paced closer. "Fancy seeing you here, *mi amor.*"

She glanced at the shovel again, wishing she was close enough to grab it.

She wasn't.

But maybe if she could buy herself some time . . .

She glanced at Freddy again. At his thin but muscular build. His thick, dark hair. His movie star smile.

Looking at him now made her feel sick to her stomach.

"How did you find us?" Her voice trembled, giving away her fear—fear that Freddy would prey on. It always seemed to empower him.

"My man Langston told me what was going on. Of course, I wanted to see for myself." He looked her up and down. "Other than the dust covering you, you're looking good."

Kota stepped back and hit the wall.

At once, she remembered the feel of Freddy's hands around her throat. She remembered the ache of painful bruises that may have faded from sight but still remained ingrained in her mind.

And what about Dean?

She still heard the grunts and moans just outside the stable.

"Just let us go," she muttered as Freddy paused in front of her.

He smirked again. "What fun would that be?"

Kota's throat tightened with fear. He had plans for her, didn't he? He'd probably been thinking about this moment since she disappeared from his life.

And whatever he had planned, it would be painful. Humiliating.

It would teach her—and anyone who dared to defy him—a lesson.

His heated gaze raked over her again. "Who's that guy with you? You're not with someone else, are you?"

He ran a finger down her cheek, outlining her face.

Her muscles instantly tensed, and her lungs seized until she could hardly breathe.

"He's a coworker," she finally said. However, deep in her heart, she knew she wanted Dean to be so much more.

"A coworker, huh?" Freddy raised an eyebrow as his finger traveled to her neck. "Funny because I feel like there's more to it than that—just from the little bits that I've heard."

"Well, you're wrong." Kota made her words sound more final. She couldn't let Freddy know about her feelings for Dean.

If Freddy thought of Dean as competition, Freddy would kill him.

She'd do whatever she could to protect Dean, just as he'd protected her throughout this ordeal.

Freddy's black, calculating gaze studied her. He didn't believe her, did he?

Jealousy—and possessiveness—marred each of his movements.

"What are you going to do?" Kota's throat burned as she asked the question.

He sneered. "I'm going to claim what's rightfully mine."

He was talking about her.

As if she were property.

If Kota went with Freddy . . . she would never leave him again except in a body bag—if that. Most likely, he'd have his guys bury her body in the desert.

Would anyone even miss her?

She trembled as she realized this Christmas truly might be her last.

CHAPTER
FIFTEEN

DEAN HEARD a deep voice sound from inside the stable.

That wasn't Jacob.

Who else was in there?

Langston used the distraction to his advantage.

He swung his fist and hit Dean in the jaw.

Dean winced.

But at least he'd gotten the man to drop the gun.

The Glock now lay somewhere in the dark street.

This fight would now be fair: fist to fist.

But he needed to get this over with.

Because something was going on in the stable.

He was sure of it.

"You may be bigger than me, but that don't mean nothin'!" Langston sprang at him again.

This time, Dean was ready.

He crouched then swung his leg beneath the man's feet.

Langston tumbled to the ground.

As he did, Dean rose, grabbed the man, and lifted him in the air.

Headfirst, he lowered Langston into an old barrel that had been left on the street.

The man's feet stuck out of the top as he kicked.

He grunted and groaned.

But he couldn't get out.

And he wouldn't be able to for a while.

Now, Dean needed to get back inside to check on Kota.

But as he stepped into the stable, he froze.

Kota was gone.

Only Jacob was there. Unmoving.

Dean quickly checked Jacob's vitals.

His heart was still beating, but barely.

They all desperately needed help right now.

He stood, his lungs tight.

Where had Kota gone?

Dean needed to find her and then they needed to get out of here . . . with Jacob.

———

Kota felt the knife pressing into her neck. She knew one wrong move and that blade would cut her skin.

Freddy led her from the stable, out a back entrance.

"You thought you could get away from me," he muttered, his breath hot on her ear. "You should have known better."

"It wasn't like that." Her voice trembled.

"Then what was it like?"

Her mind raced as she wondered how to respond. "I just wanted a new start."

"A new start without me."

"It's complicated." He'd never understand. Nothing she said would appease him. She knew that.

He grunted. "I'm sure it is."

As she glanced ahead, she saw the old Jeep in the distance.

That was how Freddy had gotten here.

Langston had probably gone back to his truck and driven until he'd found a phone signal. Then Freddy had come back here with him.

Her stomach roiled.

She'd been naive to think she could escape. That she could remain free. Of *course*, Freddy had found her. Was that even in doubt?

He had too many connections. Too many unsavory men working for him.

"What have you been doing these past two years without me, señora?" Freddy muttered as he led her to his Jeep.

The desert air—now cool and arid—swept across her, sending goosebumps over her skin.

She swallowed hard, trying to find her voice amidst her fear. "I've been working. I'm a . . . a housecleaner."

"A housecleaner? No girl of mine should be a housecleaner. You should have stuck with me. I would've given you everything you ever wanted. Vacations. Parties. Any clothes money can buy . . ."

"And I'd have bruises to wear as accessories."

"You always did have that smart mouth." He squeezed her arm harder, and she let out a yelp.

He shoved her forward until they reached the Jeep and opened the passenger door.

"Now, get in!" he snapped.

Kota knew what this meant.

If she went with him . . . this would be it.

She wouldn't be seen alive again.

At least, Dean would be safe . . . if Langston hadn't already harmed him.

But she felt certain Dean could take that man down.

"I said, get in!" Freddy yelled.

And Kota knew she had no choice but to go with him.

DEAN HAD SNEAKED around the building, toward the sound of voices in the distance.

He'd seen the Jeep parked out back and had ducked behind it.

Just in time.

As he peered over the back of the vehicle, he spotted Freddy—with a knife to Kota's throat.

Anger surged through him.

He had to help her.

But he'd have to be very careful in the process.

Freddy grabbed Kota's arm to shove her toward the Jeep again.

But as they reached the vehicle, the man lowered the knife long enough to open the passenger door.

Dean knew he had to act.

There was no time to waste.

He lunged from the shadows and tackled Freddy. The two tumbled to the ground.

Kota screamed and backed away.

"I should have handled you myself," Freddy muttered as he glared at Dean.

The man still clutched the knife as they continued to wrestle for control.

Before he could try to use it, Dean slammed the man's arm into the ground.

The knife fell from his grasp.

Kota quickly grabbed it before Freddy could reach it again.

Freddy might be smaller than Dean, but the man was spry.

"She's mine," Freddy muttered.

The next instant, he flipped Dean onto his back.

Freddy reared his head back and head-butted Dean.

Dean felt the ache pulse through his head.

Kota gasped before letting out a yell. "I won't let you hurt him!"

She raised a crowbar over her shoulder like a baseball bat. She must have found it in the Jeep.

Then she swung it toward Freddy.

The metal tip hit Freddy in the head, and he fell to the ground.

Time seemed to freeze a moment.

Dean rose and glanced at Freddy.

The man's eyes were closed, and he lay motionless.

Kota stood there a moment staring at him, almost looking breathless.

It appeared this was finally over.

———

Kota collapsed to her knees, tears pouring down her cheeks.

What had she just done? Was Freddy dead? Had she killed someone?

Dean knelt beside her and pried the crowbar from her fingers.

She hadn't realized she was still holding it.

He drew her into his arms as he murmured, "It's going to be okay."

"But . . ." She stared at Freddy.

"It's over."

"Is he . . . ?" She couldn't bring herself to finish the question.

Dean glanced beside him. "I don't think he's dead. But he'll be out of it for a while."

Relief filled her. She didn't want to take someone's life. Even if it was Freddy's.

She didn't know if she could live with herself if she did.

Dean rose and took hold of her arms. "Listen, I know you're shaken, but we need to go."

"To go?" She blinked up at him.

"We can't stay here. Let's tie these guys up, take the Jeep, and then we can find help. Jacob . . . he needs medical attention."

Kota stared at him a moment before nodding. "Okay. That . . . that sounds good."

Her entire body trembled uncontrollably, though.

She watched as Dean went to the Jeep. He flipped the headlights on before looking in the back. He returned with rope around his shoulder.

"Why did you turn on the headlights?" she asked. "Won't it run the battery down?"

"It should be fine for a few minutes. If anyone is searching for us, the lights could help them find us."

He had a good point.

He took the rope and began to wrap it around Freddy's wrists and ankles. The man moaned on the ground and stirred slightly.

Kota braced herself for any more trouble that might emerge. She couldn't let down her guard.

At that thought, a new sound filled the air.

Was that . . . ?

She didn't want to dare hope for something that wasn't true.

But as she looked up, she saw a light in the sky.

It wasn't quite the star of Bethlehem.

It was a helicopter, she realized.

It was the crew from Vanishing Ranch.

She knew they'd come looking.

Kota had felt at home with her friends at the ranch.

She'd felt like she'd found where she belonged.

And it appeared she was right.

THIRTY MINUTES LATER, the county sheriff had arrived with two ambulances.

Freddy and Langston were arrested.

Jacob was receiving medical treatment. His parents had been called and were on their way.

Dean and Kota had been given some water, crackers, and a blanket.

They'd already gone through the story of what had happened with the sheriff a couple of times.

Charlie, Ghost, and Jesse stood around them now.

"How did you find us?" Dean asked as he sat in the back of the ambulance and took another sip of his water.

"We knew something was wrong when you didn't come back in time," Charlie started. "Jesse and Monroe went out to look for you and found your truck. That's when we knew for sure that something was wrong."

"We searched the desert for a few hours and found some shell casings by the canyon," Jesse continued. "Then we found another man—he was still pulling cactus barbs off him. That guy wasn't talking. When we found the dead body in the canyon, that's when we got more people involved—including the sheriff's office."

The sheriff stepped into their conversation. "We've been trying to catch Freddy and his guys for a long time. He's started a lot of trouble in this area, and this county will be a lot safer with him behind bars."

Dean turned to Ghost. "We pulled you away from time with your girl."

The helicopter pilot shrugged. "Chesney understands. I'm just glad we found you. Glad we saw those headlights."

"Me too." Kota rubbed her arms. "Things could have turned out a lot differently."

"I'd say you're both fighters," Charlie said. "You were doing pretty well on your own. Who knows—maybe I could use you both as operatives one day."

Chef and Kota exchanged a laugh.

"I'll pass," Kota said.

"And I'll stick to cooking."

Charlie grinned and winked. "Well, let me know if you change your mind."

Everyone's gazes went to another vehicle as it pulled up in the distance.

As soon as it stopped, a man and woman climbed out.

Jacob Carlson's parents.

Their gazes instantly went to their son, and they rushed toward him, throwing their arms around him. Sobs escaped from them all.

Dean smiled, happy for their reunion.

Things could have turned out so much different.

As he glanced at his watch, he realized it was now past midnight.

That meant this rescue was a Christmas miracle.

As Charlie and her crew chatted with the sheriff a moment, Dean turned to Kota.

He'd been waiting for a second alone with her.

"You did it," he told her.

"I did what?"

"You managed to prevent any more of the evil acts that Freddy might have been planning. He won't be hurting anyone again."

She pushed a hair behind her ear and glanced at her lap. "Maybe that's true. But what about every-thing that he's already done?"

He tipped her chin up with his finger. "You were

a victim too, Kota. Maybe you survived just for this very moment—because you'd ultimately be able to help put him behind bars."

A smile slowly slid across her face. "I like that. I hope so. And I'm so glad he's no longer a threat to people. The world will be a safer place."

"Yes, it will be."

He pulled her toward him in a side hug.

She leaned against his shoulder.

Dean couldn't help but marvel at how perfect holding her felt.

Something had definitely changed between them—something he looked forward to exploring . . . later.

CHAPTER
EIGHTEEN

"WOULD YOU LOOK AT THIS?" Dean held out a platter with beautifully sliced meat on it as he stood in the Vanishing Ranch kitchen the next evening.

Kota paced closer to him and smiled as she observed the meat. "Turf flufkins."

"Turducken—" he started to correct before he realized that she was joking. A grin stretched his face instead. "Isn't it beautiful?"

"It is," Kota said. "And it smells wonderful too. I know everyone will love it. You stayed up all night to fix this, didn't you?"

He shrugged. "Maybe."

"I like your dedication, Chef—I mean, *Dean.*"

He stepped closer. "And I like the fact that you like it, Kota."

They exchanged a smile as they stood in the kitchen.

They hadn't had another moment alone—there had been too much going on.

And their day wasn't finished yet.

Kota stepped back. "Now, I have got to go get changed if I'm going to be ready in time to eat."

"You do that. The turducken will be waiting when you return. I promise." He winked.

The grin on his face didn't fade as she walked away.

It was Christmas day. Miraculously, the meat he'd purchased was still okay, thanks to a specialty cooler he'd had in his truck that kept things cold for up to twenty-four hours.

He'd worked on this meal all day, and he couldn't wait for everyone to try it.

This morning, he'd gotten an update from Charlie about their situation yesterday.

Jacob was in the hospital being treated, but he was okay. He would be headed to rehab soon in an effort to get his problems under control.

Freddy, Langston, and the third guy—the one attacked by the jumping cactus—were all in police custody. The man who'd been attacked by the mountain lion was in the hospital and in critical condition. The man who'd fallen from the cliff hadn't made it.

The good news was that these guys wouldn't be terrorizing people around here anymore.

Dean was just sorry about everything he and Kota had to go through to get to that point. Still, it looked like they'd have a happy ending.

As Dean set the platter back onto the counter, his phone rang. He glanced at the screen and saw it was his oldest son, John.

He put the device to his ear. "Merry Christmas."

"Merry Christmas to you also, Dad."

The two chatted for several moments about family and kids. John had spent Christmas with his wife's family. Dean missed seeing them, but knowing they were going to get together in January made their absence a little easier.

"Dad, I just want to let you know how proud Mom would be of you," John said.

Something caught in Dean's throat at the sound of his son's words. "What do you mean?"

"I think it's great what you're doing," John said. "You work with your whole heart, just like you always taught us. You always said that if something's worth doing, it's worth doing with everything you've got, right? That's what I see in you. You're the one who instilled that virtue in me. Right now, I can hear the joy in your voice. I know you could've gotten other jobs that paid more, but I love the fact that you're content to serve others instead."

Dean couldn't be sure, but that feeling in his throat just might be him getting choked up. "Thank you, Son. That means a lot to me."

"I mean it, Dad. You're one of a kind."

By the time Dean got off the phone, tears glistened in his eyes.

That phone call might have been one of the nicest Christmas presents he could've gotten.

If there was anything yesterday's ordeal had taught him, it was the importance of forgiveness. Not just offering it to others.

But also the importance of forgiving yourself and releasing your shame.

To trust that when the redemption story began that you were a part of it.

He busied himself getting the rest of the meal ready to serve.

To his surprise, Charlie and several other members of the crew had offered to serve and clean up for them today. They'd said he deserved a night off.

Dean had argued with them at first, but they'd insisted and had eventually won.

So when Charlie, Monroe, Jesse, and Sienna flooded the kitchen several minutes later and ushered him out, he'd been expecting it.

He quickly went back to his living quarters to shower and get ready.

When he returned to the dining hall, he paused.

A Christmas tree stood in the corner of the room. He remembered seeing the joyous expressions on the people's faces as they'd opened their gifts this morning. Fourteen guests were now staying here at the ranch—nine rescued women and their children.

Next year at this time, they hoped to have the new lodge they were building open—a lodge that would house victims of human trafficking. The operations here at Vanishing Ranch would expand and so would their responsibilities.

But Dean wouldn't have it any other way. So many needs and so little time.

This morning, he'd made a simple breakfast for the residents here—pancakes shaped like Santa Claus with some strawberries, bananas, and whipped cream.

Monroe had played the guitar, and they'd sung Christmas carols. They'd read the Christmas story from the Bible.

It almost felt like a huge extended family had gotten together to celebrate.

Everyone had fussed over Hudson and Teagan's baby boy.

Some of the staff had gone home, so not everyone was here.

But there was a true sense of camaraderie at the ranch amongst the staff and the guests.

As "I'll Be Home for Christmas" floated overhead, Dean drew in a deep breath and simply marveled at the moment. Soon, everyone would flood back inside this place to enjoy Christmas dinner. For now, he relished the quiet.

A few minutes later, Dean's eyes lit as someone stepped inside.

Kota.

She wore a long, black skirt with a fitted red top and black cowboy boots. Her long hair had big curls that stretched well beyond her shoulders. Lipstick colored her lips, and golden earrings graced her ears.

She'd never looked so beautiful—but not because of what she wore.

Because of the glow in her gaze.

She stepped toward him and grinned. "You clean up nicely."

"As do you." He reached into his pocket and pulled something out—a small, wrapped gift. "By the way, I didn't have a chance to give this to you this morning."

Her eyes widened in surprise. "What? For me?"

"Just open it."

Her hands trembled slightly as she untied the ribbon and tugged the paper apart.

Then she opened the small box.

Inside, she found the picture that they had taken in town in front of the lit-up cactus. Dean had made a small frame out of wood and put it around the photo.

"I hope the picture will bring more good memories than bad." He waited, unsure if Kota liked it or not. He couldn't read her expression.

She glanced up at him, tears in her gaze. "I love it!"

She threw her arms around his neck.

Dean felt his muscles ease as he wrapped his arms around her.

"This really has been a nice Christmas," he murmured. "Despite everything."

"Yes, it has."

Dean shifted as their gazes locked. "I've been meaning to ask . . . now that Freddy is behind bars, are you going to stay here?"

"Of course, I am. This is home."

Warmth filled him. "I was hoping you'd say that."

Kota's grin widened as she pointed above him.

Dean followed her gaze and grinned.

Mistletoe hung from the ceiling.

And he was standing right under it.

He raised his eyebrows as he looked back to her.

"Well, would you look at that. I wonder who hung that there?"

She studied his face only a moment before playfully slapping his shoulder. "You did, didn't you?"

He shrugged with another grin. "Maybe. And I may have stood right here, just in case you happened to walk in."

Laughter escaped from her. "I like the way you think."

"I like hearing that."

She stepped closer. "Since you're the one standing under it, you're supposed to be on the receiving end of this, aren't you?"

He liked the look in her eyes. "Maybe."

With another grin, Kota reached up on her tiptoes and planted a soft kiss on his lips.

More warmth flushed through him. He hoped there would be a lot more of those. But he would take it slow and follow her lead. For now, her companionship was the best gift she could give.

"Ready to try my infamous turducken?"

Her smile was all the answer that he needed.

He turned and offered his arm. "Would you like to sit together?"

"I'd love to."

"I think I should be able to arrange that. Merry Christmas, Kota."

"Merry Christmas, Dean."

The song playing from the speakers changed, and "God Rest Ye Merry Gentlemen" began to play.

As the lyrics "and tidings of comfort and joy" rang through the speakers, Dean couldn't help but marvel how true that sentiment was this Christmas season.

~~~

Thank you so much for reading *Troubled Tidings*. If you enjoyed this book, please consider leaving a review.

Stayed tuned for *Narrow Escape* coming next!
~~~

USA TODAY BESTSELLING AUTHOR
CHRISTY BARRITT
Narrow
ESCAPE
VANISHING RANCH · THE SERIES – BOOK NINE

COMPLETE BOOK LIST

Squeaky Clean Mysteries:

#1 Hazardous Duty

#2 Suspicious Minds

#2.5 It Came Upon a Midnight Crime (novella)

#3 Organized Grime

#4 Dirty Deeds

#5 The Scum of All Fears

#6 To Love, Honor and Perish

#7 Mucky Streak

#8 Foul Play

#9 Broom & Gloom

#10 Dust and Obey

#11 Thrill Squeaker

#11.5 Swept Away (novella)

#12 Cunning Attractions

#13 Cold Case: Clean Getaway

#14 Cold Case: Clean Sweep

#15 Cold Case: Clean Break

#16 Cleans to an End

While You Were Sweeping, A Riley Thomas Spinoff

The Sierra Files:

#1 Pounced

#2 Hunted

#3 Pranced

#4 Rattled

The Gabby St. Claire Diaries (a Tween Mystery series):

The Curtain Call Caper

The Disappearing Dog Dilemma

The Bungled Bike Burglaries

The Worst Detective Ever

#1 Ready to Fumble

#2 Reign of Error

#3 Safety in Blunders

#4 Join the Flub

#5 Blooper Freak

#6 Flaw Abiding Citizen

#7 Gaffe Out Loud

#8 Joke and Dagger

#9 Wreck the Halls

#10 Glitch and Famous

Raven Remington

Relentless

Holly Anna Paladin Mysteries:

#1 Random Acts of Murder

#2 Random Acts of Deceit

#2.5 Random Acts of Scrooge

#3 Random Acts of Malice

#4 Random Acts of Greed

#5 Random Acts of Fraud

#6 Random Acts of Outrage

#7 Random Acts of Iniquity

Lantern Beach Mysteries

#1 Hidden Currents

#2 Flood Watch

#3 Storm Surge

#4 Dangerous Waters

#5 Perilous Riptide

#6 Deadly Undertow

Lantern Beach Romantic Suspense

Tides of Deception

Shadow of Intrigue

Storm of Doubt
Winds of Danger
Rains of Remorse
Torrents of Fear

Lantern Beach P.D.
On the Lookout
Attempt to Locate
First Degree Murder
Dead on Arrival
Plan of Action

Lantern Beach Escape
Afterglow (a novelette)

Lantern Beach Blackout
Dark Water
Safe Harbor
Ripple Effect
Rising Tide

Lantern Beach Guardians
Hide and Seek
Shock and Awe
Safe and Sound

Lantern Beach Blackout: The New Recruits

Rocco

Axel

Beckett

Gabe

Lantern Beach Mayday

Run Aground

Dead Reckoning

Tipping Point

Lantern Beach Blackout: Danger Rising

Brandon

Dylan

Maddox

Titus

Lantern Beach Christmas

Silent Night

Crime á la Mode

Dead Man's Float

Milkshake Up

Bomb Pop Threat

Banana Split Personalities

Beach Bound Books and Beans Mysteries

Bound by Murder

Bound by Disaster

Bound by Mystery

Bound by Trouble

Bound by Mayhem

Vanishing Ranch

Forgotten Secrets

Necessary Risk

Risky Ambition

Deadly Intent

Lethal Betrayal

High Stakes Deception

Fatal Vendetta

Troubled Tidings

The Sidekick's Survival Guide

The Art of Eavesdropping

The Perks of Meddling

The Exercise of Interfering

The Practice of Prying

The Skill of Snooping

The Craft of Being Covert

Saltwater Cowboys

Saltwater Cowboy

Breakwater Protector

Cape Corral Keeper

Seagrass Secrets
Driftwood Danger
Unwavering Security

Beach House Mysteries

The Cottage on Ghost Lane
The Inn on Hanging Hill
The House on Dagger Point

School of Hard Rocks Mysteries

The Treble with Murder
Crime Strikes a Chord
Tone Death

Carolina Moon Series

Home Before Dark
Gone By Dark
Wait Until Dark
Light the Dark
Taken By Dark

Suburban Sleuth Mysteries:

Death of the Couch Potato's Wife

Fog Lake Suspense:

Edge of Peril
Margin of Error

Brink of Danger
Line of Duty
Legacy of Lies
Secrets of Shame
Refuge of Redemption

Cape Thomas Series:
Dubiosity
Disillusioned
Distorted

Standalone Romantic Mystery:
The Good Girl

Suspense:
Imperfect
The Wrecking

Sweet Christmas Novella:
Home to Chestnut Grove

Standalone Romantic-Suspense:
Keeping Guard
The Last Target
Race Against Time
Ricochet
Key Witness

Lifeline

High-Stakes Holiday Reunion

Desperate Measures

Hidden Agenda

Mountain Hideaway

Dark Harbor

Shadow of Suspicion

The Baby Assignment

The Cradle Conspiracy

Trained to Defend

Mountain Survival

Dangerous Mountain Rescue

Nonfiction:

Characters in the Kitchen

Changed: True Stories of Finding God through Christian Music (out of print)

The Novel in Me: The Beginner's Guide to Writing and Publishing a Novel (out of print)

ABOUT THE AUTHOR

USA Today has called Christy Barritt's books "scary, funny, passionate, and quirky."

Christy writes both mystery and romantic suspense novels that are clean with underlying messages of faith. Her books have sold more than three million copies and have won the Daphne du Maurier Award for Excellence in Suspense and Mystery, have been twice nominated for the Romantic Times Reviewers' Choice Award, and have finaled for both a Carol Award and Foreword Magazine's Book of the Year.

She is married to her Prince Charming, a man who thinks she's hilarious—but only when she's not trying to be. Christy is a self-proclaimed klutz, an avid music lover who's known for spontaneously bursting into song, and a road trip aficionado.

When she's not working or spending time with her family, she enjoys singing, playing the guitar, and exploring small, unsuspecting towns where people have no idea how accident-prone she is.

Find Christy online at:
www.christybarritt.com
www.facebook.com/christybarritt
www.twitter.com/cbarritt

Sign up for Christy's newsletter to get information on all of her latest releases here: **www.christybarritt. com/newsletter-sign-up/**